SPACE-AGE
TERRORS!

PLOT-YOUR-OWN
HORROR STORIES™ #3

SPACE-AGE TERRORS!

by Hilary Milton

Illustrated by Paul Frame

WANDERER BOOKS
Published by Simon & Schuster, Inc., New York

Copyright © 1983 by Hilary Milton
All rights reserved including the right of reproduction
in whole or in part in any form.
Published by WANDERER BOOKS
A Division of Simon & Schuster, Inc.
Simon & Schuster Building
1230 Avenue of the Americas
New York, New York 10020

Designed by Stanley S. Drate
Manufactured in the United States of America
10 9 8 7 6 5 4 3 2 1

WANDERER and colophon are registered trademarks
of Simon & Schuster, Inc.
PLOT–YOUR–OWN HORROR STORIES is a trademark of
Simon & Schuster, Inc.

Library of Congress Cataloging in Publication Data

Milton, Hilary H.
  Space age terrors!

  (Plot your own horror stories; 3)
  "Wanderer books."
  Summary: The reader faces a choice of unknown horrors in
the Vanguard Air, Rocket, and Space Museum after it closes,
late one night.
  [1. Horror stories. 2. Astronautical museums—Fiction. 3.
Museums—Fiction. 4. Science fiction. 5. Literary
recreations] I. Title. II. Series.
PZ7.M6447Sp 1983   [Fic]   83-9402
ISBN 0-671-49248-9 (pbk.)

BEWARE!

The Vanguard Air, Rocket, and Space Museum is filled with unnatural horror. You will struggle desperately to survive your visit there. Don't read straight through, however, as every time you think you're safe, a new and frightening choice will have to be made.

Where do you think the giant monkey and the huge tarantula spider are taking you?

Will you survive your ordeal in the g-force simulator column?

Should you seek safety from the evil robot soldiers in a helicopter loaded with explosive missiles?

Can you get out of the Gemini spacecraft or will you be propelled into outer space?

Remember that your fate is in your own hands. Only you can decide whether or not you'll make it through the many hair-raising tales in SPACE-AGE TERRORS!

For the past five days you and your parents have been sightseeing in California. Now, as you lie in the motel bed across the room from where your mother and father are sleeping, all sorts of images are flitting through your thoughts.

Last Saturday you flew from your home in Cleveland, Ohio, to San Diego. There, your father rented a car and the *real* trip began. You toured the fantastic San Diego Zoo, with all of its exotic animals. Then you drove straight up to Disneyland, where you spent two days. The Sleeping Beauty Castle was so beautiful you thought you were dreaming. You also enjoyed watching the parade, then visiting Frontierland. The best part, though, came when the Mickey Mouse character put his arm around your shoulder.

From Disneyland, you traveled to Los Angeles and took a bus tour of Hollywood and Beverly Hills. While there, you were sure you saw two movie stars. One of them, you think, was Robert Mitchum, and you're pretty sure the woman was Elizabeth Taylor.

After leaving Los Angeles, you traveled north past Vandenburg Air Force Base, and this afternoon you spent a long time visiting the Vanguard Air, Rocket, and Space Museum.

Turn to page 2.

2

Of all the places you visited, this one was the most fascinating. You saw full-scale models—they're called mock-ups—of satellites and all sorts of space capsules. On special display were three manned space vehicles—one from the Project Mercury, the first manned space-flight program; one from Gemini; and one from Apollo, the lunar orbit mission. And there were more kinds of rockets than you believed ever existed.

Several people were in the party with you, and as the museum guide stopped at each display to explain specific details, people would ask questions. The guide had said that after more than twenty years of space activity, there had to be a lot of junk floating above the earth. A high-school student then jokingly asked if there were any astronauts. The guide paused and glanced at him, then pointed to the far corner of the huge museum. Hanging high above from the ceiling was a space vehicle unlike anything else you'd seen. It was almost round, except that one side seemed to have been cut off or flattened. On the end opposite the flat side was a high knob, about twice the size of a man's head.

"That is a *Vostok*—a mock-up of a Soviet satellite," the guide had said. "The Soviets deny it, but we believe that one of their cosmonauts was performing EVA—extra-vehicular activities—and was outside the space capsule when his life support tether broke. He was lost."

Turn to page 3.

3

Lost in space, you think.

While you were in the museum you also saw some old airplanes, a helicopter gunship used in Vietnam, all sorts of space suits, some plants that had grown from seeds taken up into space, and one small rhesus monkey that had been taken on one of the first lunar laboratory missions. You also walked past two rooms with thick greenish-glass doors; one was marked AUTHORIZED PERSONNEL ONLY and the other was DO NOT ENTER.

By the time you and your parents checked into the motel two blocks from the space museum, you were too tired to do any more sightseeing.

Now, though, as you turn from side to side on the motel bed, you can't sleep. You keep thinking about the zoo animals, the buildings and people of Disneyland, and the strange space hardware. When you finally doze off, you don't rest comfortably. Instead, you have crazy dreams. In one, you're riding a lion at the zoo, chasing an ostrich. In another, you're sitting on the top of the Sleeping Beauty Castle, watching as a satellite is being launched.

The most fearful dream, though, is different. You are at Disneyland and one of the Disney characters comes up to you and whispers, "Let's take a special, secret ride." You follow, and the two of you climb into a missile-shaped device and lie down. The character—Pluto?—touches a switch. At once, you hear a terrible

Turn to page 4.

4

roar. You smell fire and smoke, the device begins to vibrate, and before you know it you're launched into space.

The dream is so terrifying that it wakes you up. You sit up, stare toward the motel window—and suddenly remember something. Your camera. You've lost your camera.

You think hard. You start to wake up your parents. And then you remember that you left it in the space museum. You put it on the seat beside you while you were watching the film showing the first launch of the space shuttle *Columbia*.

You've got to get it back because it still has all the pictures in it of all the great things you saw today. But you can't wait till morning—your father said you were going to leave real early, before the museum opened.

You quickly slip out of bed and into your clothes. It is just a short walk to the museum. A guard can let you in to get the camera and return without waking up your parents.

Five minutes later, you are at the door to the museum—but you don't see a guard. You knock on the heavy glass door. Nobody answers. You knock again. Still no response.

But there has to be somebody here!

You grab the heavy door handle and give it a shake—and make a startling discovery. Somebody forgot to lock it!

Turn to page 5.

Good, you think to yourself. You'll just slip inside, scurry past the ticket desk and souvenir shop, then go to the theater just off the main hallway.

The inside is dimly lit with little green lights. You go past the water fountain and turn toward the huge museum room. You move slowly in the dim light because you don't want to trip.

You reach the second turn and are close to the theater door when you hear a sudden noise. You think it is a door being opened. And then you hear footsteps.

If you think you've attracted a guard's attention, turn to page 24.
If you believe your father has followed you, turn to page 18.
But if the sound may be something different, turn to page 12.

6

The sight of those two huge creatures coming toward you makes you want to run away quickly.

Horrified, you spin about and start to stand. But before you can do more than get to your knees, the spider fixes its stare on you and spits.

A fleck of moisture strikes your wrist and suddenly burns you. Before you can so much as wipe at the spot, however, you feel a frightening numbness spread up your arm and across your shoulder. You can move, but your motions are dulled.

The two continue to move toward you, and when they are beside you, the monkey, still baring its teeth, reaches out with its other forepaw and catches you by the neck. It lifts you, and you are forced to your feet. Before you can move again, the creature clasps your hand.

And the three of you begin to move toward the main museum room.

You reach it and turn toward the rocket section. While you are crossing the floor you hear a harsh noise. You glance to the right. You spot one of the soldier dummies, which you vaguely remember seeing during the tour. This one is dressed in combat uniform, shouldering a rocket gun. The guide had told you these rockets fired laser beams and could disable a tank by destroying all of its electrical systems.

If this is your chance to escape, turn to page 27.
Or will you be caught between the creatures and the
soldier? Turn to page 34.

8

Cautiously, you rise enough to peep over the top of the case. The spider has jumped to its top and is now frantically at work weaving a peculiar web. Judging from the size of this creature, you believe its web will be unusually strong. Strong enough to capture you?

The thought terrifies you and you squat low, turning toward the other objects on display, searching for another place to hide. You spot the large moon-shaped chamber, which the guide had called an astrodome, with a small entry. A person could go inside, close the door, lie on a special couch, and see what space looks like, much as an astronaut on the moon would see it. According to the guide, the couch revolves slowly, the overhead "sky" within the astrodome also moves, and you get the real sensation of being there.

You didn't get inside during the tour, and you're not so sure you care to see the universe from a turning couch. But if you can get inside the astrodome and close the door, it'll be a safe place to hide.

You take a deep breath, glance one more time at the web, and scamper across the floor to the astrodome.

You open the door and step inside . . . .

Turn to page 79.

You and the giant rhesus are floating in outer space in the Gemini capsule.

You cannot guess what the big monkey will do, but you are sure the creature will do something unexpected. You try to imagine what other controls are at your fingertips, which ones are nearest the monkey's seat. But this is one thing the guide hadn't mentioned.

You think of all the possibilities—guidance, speed, spacecraft position, ejection—

No! Not ejection in space!

9

Turn to page 63.

10

You think you're in a research laboratory.

You shake your head and stare in the direction of the row of cages. You spot a creature that looks like a mouse, except it is much larger than a cat! You spy a frog, but it is as big and round as a lopsided volley ball! You think you see a spider, but it is much, much bigger than the largest tarantula you've ever seen pictured!

For a moment you try to understand. Then it slowly dawns on you. During some of the missions, you know the astronauts took certain live plants and animals into space to see what the strange environment would do to them. You've never read about these creatures, though. However, you suspect the experiments produced very unexpected results.

You start to get up when you hear a cage door swing open at the farthest end of the room. You turn quickly and spot a creature almost as large as you letting itself out of its cage. You swallow hard. You remember the tiny rhesus monkey in its museum display cage and you realize this creature looks exactly like that one, except for the size.

You gulp because suddenly you know what happened. The space environment made terrible changes in the tiny rhesus, and this is its offspring, its huge offspring!

If you believe there is cause for concern, turn to page 19.
If you think you'd better stay motionless, turn to page 31.

You're not sure what went wrong, but the spacecraft is now trembling violently.

And then you remember. This is not a real space rocket. It is a mock-up—something that looks and acts like the real thing. But it is a lot smaller. It doesn't have everything a real one has. It has controls, rockets, instruments, and seats.

But it does not have one thing—one very important thing.

It does not have a parachute!

You swallow hard. No parachute—no safe landing. It does not matter whether you're over land or water because you're about to crash.

But you don't crash. You do hit water. And within seconds the spacecraft sinks to the bottom of Lake Michigan. And it will never float to the surface . . . .

THE END

12

You see a shadowy figure moving toward you, making no effort to walk softly. Good, you're thinking, it'll be the night watchman. You'll just tell him why you're in the museum so late, let him help you find your camera, then you'll run back to the motel. But when he approaches, you suddenly realize this is no night watchman. This man isn't a guard, either. He is too tall, much too tall.

When he gets within fifteen feet of where you're standing, you realize that he is the tallest man you have ever seen. His head almost touches the ceiling of the passageway, and you know that is at least ten feet.

He is wearing an astronaut's helmet and space suit, but there is something very peculiar about the suit's color. The ones you remember seeing on display were white, except for the one that was silver, but it wasn't a real one; it was used in a movie.

This giant creature's space suit is a glowing orange.

Is it a robot? Turn to page 51.
Is it a special kind of astronaut? Turn to page 53.

The sight of the two creatures walking toward you horrifies you. Besides, you always thought tarantulas were deadly enemies of animals as well as people. But the monkey and the spider seem to be getting along together just fine.

13

It's all too weird.

You get to your knees, putting one hand against the door, and slowly stand. They pause. You draw back a hand as if you had something to throw. The giant monkey begins to dance up and down and the spider darts left, then right. You think they'll both scamper away if you run toward them. You set yourself, take a deep breath, let out a war cry, and lunge forward.

The spider leaps straight up—so high that you run underneath it. The monkey drops to all fours and scampers to the side. And you think you have gotten away. But just as you are beginning to feel relieved, you hear something strike the hard floor with a spat. You look back.

The spider has spread out and is much larger than before. Its huge, bulging eyes have turned a firelike red. Its body begins to change colors—first brown, then blue, then a glowing yellow.

The terrible eyes roll about for a moment, then they stare straight into yours.

Turn to page 93.

14

The space-suited robot stops walking about ten feet in front of you and points a glowing finger at you.

Sparks start to flash from it, and they get longer and longer. You remember seeing some of the complex electronic devices astronauts use for working on space vehicles. This may be one of them, but it looks like a special heating device that might be used for welding.

The sparks become long fire-darts, and one of them suddenly flicks at your finger.

Your next thought is that the robot, or whatever this thing in the space suit is, means to burn you.

Turn to page 68.

15

You stand as still as you can, daring not to breathe. The monkey has obviously been around humans, but you have no idea how it behaves.

It reaches to where you are standing, pauses, looks you over, then slowly walks around you, gesturing with its left forepaw. You do not move. When it reaches your right side, it gently touches your hand. You want to jerk your hand away but are afraid that any quick movement might make it do something frightening.

Turn to page 76.

16

Perhaps if you push the door marked DO NOT ENTER it will open, but you can't take time to find out. One look at the approaching robot tells you you can't stand there any longer. You spin about and rush headlong up the corridor toward the high-ceilinged main area of the museum. You pause long enough for your eyes to become accustomed to the near darkness, then you glance to the left. Sitting there is the Project Mercury manned space vehicle with its one tiny seat, cramped quarters, and—yes—its open cockpit area where the windshield/heatshield had been. You make a quick decision and dash toward it, scrambling through the small opening, twisting about, and slumping in the pilot's seat. As you do so, you wonder how a grown man of John Glenn's size could have fitted into the cramped space.

You scrunch down, knowing the robot is still lumbering in your direction. You place your arms on the armrests . . .

And without warning, metal straps click up and into place.

You are now handcuffed to the arms!

You start to yell, then catch yourself because you don't want the robot to know where you're hiding. You feel about in the dark, hoping to find the release lever—there just has to be one!

If you think the lever you find is the correct one, turn to page 23.

If you hesitate when you find the lever, turn to page 40.

The sign on the door says DO NOT ENTER, but you don't care. It is probably an office, anyway. You put your shoulder against it and shove as hard as you can. It yields much easier than you had guessed it would—and you fall through, sprawling on the floor. The door swings shut at once, and you hear a click that you assume is simply a loose latch.

17

Before you have time to think about *that* noise, however, you hear others—very different ones. You think you hear the low chatter and whimper of a baby. Then you think you hear a hissing noise. You *know* you hear the throaty sound of a frog. And you believe you distinguish the squeak of a mouse, although it is deeper than the squeak of any mouse you've ever heard.

Most important of all, however, you hear many soft, padded movements.

All around you there is a faint green glow, and you have to adjust your vision to the dimmer lights. You peer about and discover you're in a special kind of room much like you've seen back home where a motel for pets boards small animals.

Animals?

If you believe you're in a research laboratory, turn to page 10.

If you believe this is a veterinarian's office attached to the air, rocket, and space museum, turn to page 28.

18

The sound from the door opening has an echo, and you feel certain it is the one you used to enter the museum. You are thinking it is your father because he heard you and got up to see where you were going.

You turn around, hesitate a moment, then decide you might as well tell him the truth.

Except that when the figure comes into sight, you can see it is not your father. It is one of the guards. You know he'll catch you, perhaps accuse you of breaking in, and probably call the police.

And you don't want to answer police questions.

Turn to page 99.

The prospect of what these creatures are is very frightening. If they are so much larger than they should be, they might also be able to hurt you, maybe even kill you.

The thought scares you even more. You don't want to face that robot, but you surely don't want to be attacked by these terrible creatures.

While you are still sprawled on the floor, the giant rhesus slams its cage door shut, rocks side to side, and gives its head a little shake. Its lips spread, almost in a grin, and it bares white, wicked-looking teeth. For a moment you think it is coming for you. But no—instead, it scampers to the other cages and opens all the barred gates. The huge frog waddles to the edge, croaks once, then leaps halfway across the room, plopping on the floor inches from your head. The mouse eases out, sniffs, and squeaks twice. And the spider crawls across the floor of its cage, makes what appears to be a short web, and lowers itself to the floor. As it faces you, its bulbous eyes glow a brilliant orange.

And when all are free, the huge monkey turns toward you.

Turn to page 32.

20

You suppose they're intended to represent some aspect of space flight, but something has gone wrong. They should not be so firelike. They should not dart so close to the chair. And they should not touch you.

But they do! They begin to strike you as if they were tiny balls of acid fire. One hits your arm. Another hits you on the cheek. And when you turn aside, one of them strikes your ear.

You frantically hit the control panel again. You press a large switch, and all at once you are no longer in the chair. You are being jerked forward by a terrifying magnetic force. You strike the screen, but you do not feel it. You are absorbed by it. And in the twinkling of an eye, you're no longer observing the simulator because you're a part of it. And you know, as you begin to move with the screen, that you are in a magnetic blanket of stars, and it will never let you go . . . .

THE END

Right now, however, you don't care about rockets. All you want to do is get down and get out of this place!

You glance about anxiously and spot a rope ladder—the kind helicopter pilots sometimes use when they want to let a passenger down or pick up someone without having to land. You grab the first rung, hold the door open, and drop the ladder. Without waiting to see where the robot is, you scramble down, turn to the left, and spot a low window. You don't care whether it is locked or not. You run toward it. Pausing long enough to take off a shoe, you hit the window pane.

It sets off a terrifying alarm, but it breaks! That is all that matters. You scramble through, find yourself outside, and run as hard as you can toward the street leading back to the motel. And you do not stop until you're back inside, in bed, breathing hard, and knowing you can wait till tomorrow for the camera. You don't want to lose it, but you think you'd rather do that than be caught by that robot . . . .

THE END

22

And that is weird. Monkeys can't make plans, and neither can spiders. But you feel certain that—whatever they can or cannot do—these two brought you to this spot with a plan in mind.

You have no intention of becoming a part of their scheme. You'll get away, but you have to do it just right.

You stare at the rocket model. And you begin to tremble. Your body shakes all over, and your hand slowly jerks free of the monkey's paw. It seems not to care, and that is just what you want it to do. You start to lean forward as if you want to take a closer look at the manned capsule. The spider moves to the side. The monkey turns about, beginning to jabber, and for the moment it ignores you.

You glance toward the left. There, just beyond the display case filled with tiny particles from the moon, you spot the lunar lander, the mock-up of the vehicle that men used to land on the moon. A low ladder is set up beside it so tourists can climb up and look inside. And it has a door.

That is what you remember—it has a door.

But just as you set yourself for a sudden dash, the spider springs straight up and lands on top of your head.

Turn to page 82.

23

Your groping fingers touch something round and long. It has to be a lever of some sort. You clasp it, twist hard, then tug with all the strength you can muster in that cramped position.

Nothing happens.

You attempt to turn it but it does not turn. You pull as hard as you can pull. It does not move. You become frantic. You may have gotten away from that robot for a few moments, but you know it'll keep stalking you. And you're a captive victim now.

You twist to the left—and as you do so your thumb slips to the very top of the lever. You find a large button there. Of course, there is usually a safety button on levers! You press it at once, trying to move the lever at the same time. The lever slides forward, and suddenly the space capsule begins to spin.

That's not what you want! You don't care what it might have been like with the astronauts—all you want to do is escape.

You struggle hard and shove the lever the opposite way. Abruptly, the manned capsule stops spinning and begins bouncing as if it is mounted on motorized springs. You feel like you're going to be jostled to death. Every time it bounces, your head bangs against the hard headrest.

Never mind the robot—you start to scream!

Turn to page 102.

24

You stand perfectly still, not even daring to breathe. The steps are slow, much too slow to be those of a guard. And you can't see any light—a guard would certainly have a flashlight. You swallow hard and turn slowly toward your left. There is very little light, but you cannot believe what your squinting eyes see. One of the space suits you saw on display earlier is no longer within its glass case. The noise you heard first—that sounded like a door opening—wasn't a door at all but one of the glass partitions.

You swallow hard. It cannot be! A space suit just cannot move all by itself!

But it is, and as you stare at the suit, it makes a sharp right turn and heads straight for you. You stare hard. Your gaze fixes on the thick green mask that covers the astronaut's face. You see two glowing red lights right where eyes should be.

You remember that some of the suits had dummies in them—like store mannequins—but not one of them was worn by a human.

Perhaps it is some sort of robot—a robot dressed in space garb. But whatever it is, it appears to be moving directly at you. And in that instant you are sure of one thing. It is not going to be friendly.

It stops within ten feet of where you're standing, raises its right arm, and points a finger at you. The fingertip begins to glow.

Turn to page 14.

But it does something, causing the space capsule to rotate very slowly to the left. It does not stop until you've been turned 180 degrees, and you're now facing the floor instead of the museum's ceiling.

It isn't just the floor, however—you're looking down at a series of criss-crossed bars much like a grill. You cannot understand what it is for, but right now you don't have time to wonder. For you can hear the robot coming closer—its heavy feet are thumping across the museum floor.

But for the moment it cannot see you.

You twist both hands and discover that once the space capsule is inverted, the straps release of their own accord. And you are free to leave the astronaut's seat.

You ease through the now upside-down windshield opening very cautiously and let yourself down onto the grill.

And then you scream!

Turn to page 83.

26

You think the rocket was called a Viper or maybe a Stinger. But that doesn't matter now. You remember that the description said it could knock out an armored tank. Anything that powerful could destroy most of the exhibits within the museum.

You don't know what the robot soldier intends, but you do not wish to find out. You glance hastily to your left, but the wall is in that direction. You turn to your right and spot a small room the guide had said was a moon orbit test device. You don't remember what else he had said about it, but there is a door. If you can get to it, perhaps the robot won't follow. You watch it until you think its attention is directed the opposite way, then you spin about and scamper toward the door. The knob turns easily. You dart through the opening and close the door.

Almost instantly you realize something within the test device is moving. And you're caught in the motion!

Turn to page 111.

This might be your chance to escape, but the soldier dummy is no longer a "dummy." It is moving about, slowly turning in your direction. You see the laser rocket being raised to the figure's shoulder. And you know something most peculiar is about to happen.

The monkey begins to jabber, its lips spread and its teeth open and close. The spider stretches on its four hind legs, its four front legs pawing the air.

The soldier figure takes aim and fires.

The monkey drops to its belly, but the spider scampers to the side. It takes refuge behind the support post holding up a counter display.

Once more the soldier takes aim. This time the laser gun is aimed directly at you.

You glance down at the monkey—only to discover that it is slowly disintegrating and disappearing.

Have you escaped one fate, only to be caught by another? Turn to page 38.
Or can you avoid the soldier? Turn to page 44.

28

The smells, though, tell you that it is more than a place for boarding pets. You believe it is a place where sick creatures are brought, except why would they have sick animals at this museum?

You think hard, and suddenly you know why! They don't have sick animals here. These are animals which the space scientists experiment with.

Your eyes grow accustomed to the dim light and you look around. Your first impression appears to be correct. You see small chairs, small cots, and special restraining devices along the far wall, with electronic wires and cables attached to each one.

But whatever they are, this is not the way out of the museum or toward the theater. You start to turn, but suddenly a strong light flicks on and you are bathed in its brilliant glow. You blink, you cover your eyes, then you peer down. At a desk you had not seen at first there is a bald-headed man with thick glasses. Scattered papers are before him, but he is now staring at you. And there is something ominous in the way he stares.

Turn to page 97.

You swallow hard and attempt to scream. But the windshield closes with a snap, and you're a captive within the spacecraft.

You hear a second hum, and within seconds you sense a change in your position. The gantry is activated and you know the mock-up rocket is being raised, just like a real one, into firing position.

And suddenly you realize what is about to happen. This thing is a real rocket! The monkey has activated the systems! And within seconds there'll be—

No! No, no, no, no!

But you are powerless.

As the rocket rises from horizontal to vertical, you look up and see that a gaping hole has opened in the museum ceiling. You try to struggle against the straps, but the stupor caused by the spider's poison keeps you from moving.

Will you launch or not? Turn to page 50.
If you're ever going to escape, you have to do it soon.
Turn to page 36.

30

Although the robot is still stalking you, you realize one thing: in that space suit it cannot run as fast as you can. And, being so large, it cannot slip into very small places.

Without wasting a second you whirl about and run toward the museum's main passageway again, knowing only that you have to find a place to hide. You reach the main floor, glance all about, and rush toward a ladder at the far side. You grab the fourth rung and climb to the top. There is a small door and you open it. Without stopping to see where you are, you fall through and let the door shut behind you. Only then do you take a deep breath and look about.

And you shake all over. You feel you have made a mistake. You've climbed aboard that mock-up Russian space ship—the copy of the *Vostok*. Bright lights flood the area. You glance around and realize that this full-scale model has all the space instruments that the Russians might have used—except the labels are in their language.

Well, at least that robot can't find you. You'll stay here for a while until it goes somewhere else, then ease out and get your camera. You think that won't take long.

Turn to page 92.

31

Both fascinated and frightened, you dare not move. You don't want to attract the creature's attention. Once the giant monkey is standing free from the cage, it puts its forearms down with its paws on its hips, much like a person trying to decide what to do next. It glances about at the other cages, then it opens its lips and makes a soft, grunting noise. It walks to the cage where the spider is, pauses, pokes at the creature, makes a sound like a laugh, then jumps back as the spider springs to its cage's side mesh. The big monkey scratches itself under its arms, jumps lightly up and down, then turns and lets out a very mournful sigh.

Turn to page 81.

32

You are sprawled on the floor of the laboratory with this huge rhesus monkey staring at you.

And the gigantic spider turns toward you.

And the oversized mouse looks at you, its beady eyes glowing green.

You tremble all over and slowly move your arms. You know you don't want to stay here any longer, but you don't want to make any sudden move that will startle them into attacking you. Cautiously, you ease to your feet, wait until you're sure you have good balance, then you whirl about and charge for the door.

It does not open.

And you're trapped!

With a little cry, you back up, set your shoulders, and once more charge for the door. You must be stronger than you thought, for this time the door bangs open so hard that its hinges bend. It won't close. But you don't care—you're out of that room!

If you think you'd be safe in another room, turn to page 46.

If you think getting out of the museum is more important, turn to page 39.

The robot is still ten or fifteen feet away, though, and you know you can run faster than it can stalk. Remembering those two doors you saw when you visited the place earlier today, the ones marked DO NOT ENTER and AUTHORIZED PERSONNEL ONLY, you whirl to the left and race along the narrow, carpeted path toward the first one. When you reach it, you grab for the knob—only to discover there isn't one.

33

If you believe the door is unlocked, turn to page 17.
If you believe it is smarter to run in another direction, turn to page 16.

34

You don't know what the soldier dummy means to do, but you do know that you're trapped between him and the creatures. You look from him to the monkey and are about to drop to the floor, hoping to escape both. Just then the spider suddenly releases its grip on the monkey's paw and darts forward. Within three feet of the soldier, it rears up on its hind legs, wiggles its long feelers, and spits again.

The soldier with the laser gun suddenly and completely evaporates!

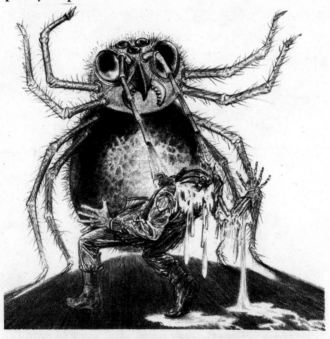

Turn to page 104.

You're terrified, but you know that if you panic, you won't ever see home again. You take a deep breath, trying to remember what you've read about the early space flights. The astronauts, you remember, did not land on earth but splashed down in the ocean. They had huge parachutes attached to the spacecraft.

35

Swallowing hard and ignoring the wild chattering of the big monkey, you scan the control panels. You see instruments that indicate various kinds of maneuvers to keep the spacecraft in proper orbit; others indicate the altitude and speed, and one set of controls marked RE-ENTRY SYSTEMS.

Re-entry. That is what you have to consider. You strain, trying to read the individual controls: RETRO-ROCKETS, PARACHUTE DEPLOYMENT, SPACECRAFT ATTITUDE FOR HEAT SHIELD AND RE-ENTRY ATTITUDE.

But you don't know in what order they're used!

Turn to page 74.

36

The rocket reaches a vertical position, and you're now lying on your back with your legs over the edge of the chair. But *you don't want to be launched into space!*

You wildly feel about, hoping to find your own set of controls. And luckily, you do. Your groping finger touches a large round button. You don't know what it is supposed to do, but you press it with all your strength.

The rocket vibrates with a violent rocking motion. It tilts backward, forward, to the left, then to the right. The monkey begins screaming. It flails its arms back and forth, its long tail flitting about like a rope in a strong wind. And accidentally that tail strikes another switch. The windshield flies off and falls to the museum floor. The monkey is ejected and sent spinning across the room. The straps holding you in place become unsnapped.

And you fall free, but you're *not* free!

You fall right beside the tarantula, which is now very agitated. It springs straight up, its legs spread wide, and when it comes down, it lands on your chest. Its weird head bends close, its horrid mouth opens, and those glowing bulbous eyes fix on just the right spot . . . .

THE END

38

You're thinking that you've just escaped from the two animal monsters only to be vaporized by a laser-wielding soldier "dummy."

You frantically look right and left, wishing for a way to elude the soldier. Suddenly you hear a light scraping sound nearby, and you glance down. The spider has eased to the side of the post where it was hiding and now is in position to see the soldier. And it is as if the creature has the ability to reason! It sets itself in an aiming position, squats down, and . . .

It spits at the dummy!

Turn to page 73.

You can only think of getting out of the museum.

You hesitate for only a moment before making a sharp turn to your left and racing toward the main door of the museum. If you knocked open that laboratory door, what could keep you from knocking open the big one?

You reach it, pausing to brace yourself, then bang against it. Unlike the one leading to the animal room, however, this door is much heavier. Wincing from the pain in your shoulder, you fall backward, slamming your elbow against the hard tile floor. Now your whole arm is throbbing. You start to get up when you glance back in the direction of the laboratory from where you had just escaped.

And you don't like what you see!

The monkey and the spider are coming out side by side. The monkey's forepaw is clinging to one of the spider's feelers. And both are coming toward you!

Do you think you can run away? Turn to page 6.
Or can you make them run? Turn to page 13.

40

You let your fingers rest on the lever that is located at the end of the left armrest. You start to turn it to the right, then you catch yourself. Maybe it won't release you. But you have to do something!

Turn to page 91.

41

Very cautiously, you ease up until you are standing at the end of the display. And you feel relieved. Just as you'd thought, you've disturbed the items in the case, and one of the hands has fallen on its side.

You peer around the corner of the case and you realize the spider is not looking directly in your direction. Good. You glance right and left, quickly spy a huge round column, chance a hurried look toward the spider, and dart from the case toward the column. You remember it from the earlier tour. The guide had said it was some kind of test device used to determine how many g-forces an astronaut could safely take. He had opened a small door at the column's base, showing that it was more like a hollow, vertical tube with a padded reclining chair at the bottom. An astronaut would get in the seat and strap himself into position. An electric elevator would slowly lift the chair up and then suddenly release it. A small motor began accelerating the chair as it fell. And by the time it reached the bottom of the column, which reached all the way to the museum's ceiling, the passenger would be traveling at 100 mph.

And he would stop suddenly!

Turn to page 98.

42

You don't care what kind of rockets they are—all you want to do is climb onto the helicopter to keep from falling to the floor. You reach around and grab the door frame. Struggling, you pull yourself inside the helicopter and fall onto the canvas-covered seat.

Leaning forward, you see the space robot, still moving across the museum floor. It seems to pause and look at the Mercury capsule. Then, as if it knows exactly what has happened, it turns its helmeted head up and stares directly at the helicopter. It raises one arm, takes aim, and darts of lightninglike sparks zing upward. One of them strikes the nose of the helicopter. One seems to strike the rotor—it *did* strike the rotor!

And suddenly the rotor begins to turn.

You catch your breath. All you need now is to have a runaway gunship roaring inside the museum.

The roar becomes a high-speed whine, and you feel the entire helicopter vibrate. It lifts from its moorings and begins to rise toward the museum ceiling.

But you know it can go only so far!

Turn to page 113.

43

Instantly, the top of the space vehicle flies open and you're catapulted—chair and all—upward. Once you're out of the spacecraft, the chair armrests release you, and you are flying through the air—above most of the displayed objects.

You frantically flail your arms, hoping to grasp something that will keep you from plunging to the floor. Your right hand contacts something hard; you grab onto it and cling with all your might.

It is the side door to the suspended Huey helicopter gunship—the one you saw earlier in the day—the kind they used in the Vietnam war. It has two rocket pods, one on the right side and another on the left. These pods are loaded with combat rockets.

If you believe the rockets work, turn to page 42.
If you believe there is a way down, turn to page 21.

44

You are trying to figure out a way of avoiding the deadly soldier "dummy."

Once more you turn your frantic gaze toward the soldier. Although you still feel the sting from the spider's poison, you force yourself to raise your hand. "Stop!" you think that you yell.

But not a sound comes out of your mouth.

You wave and try to shake your head. You attempt to drop to your knees. But there is little motion—it is as if everything you try to do fails.

The soldier seems to laugh. But he makes no sound either. His arms hold the rocket out so that you can almost look into its long, round barrel.

He fires again.

Again, there is a flash of light.

And you feel the blow of fire in the middle of your forehead. For a moment you continue to stand. Then, as your senses become numb, you crumple to the floor.

Your last thought is that the spider will survive . . . .

THE END

46

You must seek refuge in another room.

Without a backward glance, you turn right and scamper along the passageway and do not stop until you come to a small door. It should be open because you remember it from the tour; the guide had told you that behind it was a special space-voyage simulator. You grab the small knob, jerk open the narrow door, and slip inside. The door closes with a whispering swoosh.

The small simulator is much darker than the other rooms, and for a moment you think it is totally without lights. But as your eyes become accustomed to the dark space, you see little blinking lights all around you. Then you realize that the room is like a ball and you're inside it. You feel around and find a small chair—and decide you'll take a short rest. You ease yourself down, sigh, and start to relax.

You let your left hand fall to your side, but suddenly wish you had not done so. For your fingers touch small push-button switches, and before you can control yourself, you begin to feel quite dizzy.

And you know why. The chair begins to sway from side to side while the screen with the blinking lights starts to revolve.

You frantically feel for the panel where the button is and hit another switch. At once, little flashes of light dart from the screen, and you know they're electrically charged.

Turn to page 20.

47

Heat-seeking rocket?! You tremble all over because you know your body gives off heat. You don't know how much heat the rocket needs in order to search out its target, but you do not intend to find out. Not tonight!

You hesitate a moment, take a deep breath, then you whirl around and dash in the direction opposite from where the robot soldier is.

But it doesn't matter. The sound of your footsteps is all it needs. You hear a whirring noise as if something was launched, and just as you drop to the floor, a rocket whistles by, barely missing your head.

You cry out and roll across the floor, hoping to find some kind of display to hide behind. You reach the heavy concrete-supported piece of machinery called an accelerator simulator. The concrete, you believe, is large and heavy enough to stop one of those rockets.

The robot fires again. You hear the rocket whistle through the air. It strikes the concrete support . . . .

Turn to page 103.

48

The oversized rhesus monkey begins jumping around, scurrying from one end of the rocket to the other, dragging you along. With its lips wide open and its teeth shining in the dim light, it grunts and touches the manned capsule window.

Can the creature be thinking? It seems to be.

It clasps a small knob and pulls. The windshield opens, revealing two compact seats, side by side. The monkey gestures and you know it means for you to climb in. But you do not want to enter. You struggle, attempting to free your hand from its grasp. But before you do so, the huge tarantula spits once more. You feel a vicious sting just above the ankle. You immediately go limp.

The monkey drags you over the side and plops you into one of the seats. It is too small, but there is nothing you can do about it. As soon as you're in, the monkey straps you down, then clambers into the other seat. You don't like it but you're almost paralyzed from the spider's poison.

Jabbering in its excitement, the monkey pulls a space helmet over your head, then places another on itself. Its paws flounder about, then one of them clasps a round knob. It tugs, and you suddenly hear a humming noise.

Turn to page 29.

You don't know what the creature did, but you shove one of the controls as hard as you can, hoping it will stop the vibrations.

But nothing happens.

You pull the control lever again, but still nothing. It seems not to move at all. You shift your hand from that particular lever to another one, to the left of the first. You pull on it, but it does not move. You push against it. It still doesn't move. You try to move it right, then left. It remains stuck.

Your mouth gets dry. Your tongue sticks to your lips. And your heart is pounding too rapidly. With frantic motions, you move your hand from the first control, then to another, then to a third. Not one of them budges!

You kick your feet trying to locate the foot controls. Your feet find them, but they, like the hand controls, do not respond.

The monkey turns this way and that, still pounding at the windshield. Its right paw reaches up and hits one of the buttons on the upper panel. All of a sudden you hear a strange, whistling noise.

Turn to page 87.

50

The rocket reaches a vertical position. You hear creaking as the gantry swings free. The gigantic rhesus chatters even more loudly, its forepaws flapping about and its tail swinging rapidly back and forth. One of its paws comes to rest on a large lever, and its chatter suddenly stops. It turns to look at you, its lips now tightly closed. It grunts once, then it jerks the lever.

A mighty roar follows!

You cannot believe what you're hearing, but you've heard that violent noise on television—the rockets are firing! Thick clouds of billowing smoke erupt and flood the museum. And you begin to lift off.

Up, up, up, up.

Turn to page 80.

Could this creature in a glowing orange space suit be a robot?

With a couple of quick steps, you get to the passage wall and press against it, making yourself as flat as possible. The figure continues to move. But as you watch it, you realize something very peculiar. Although its feet touch the floor and you distinctly hear footsteps, they don't seem to be coming at precisely the same time.

But whatever this thing is, you know you don't want any part of it.

It reaches where you are standing, pauses briefly, then continues its march. It heads for one of the large glass display cases, not slowing down at all, and just walks right through it.

It walks through it, but does not break it!

You swallow hard, then your attention shifts to the far wall of the museum.

A green light flickers—a crazy green light.

Turn to page 57.

52

You're thinking that the whole spacecraft is breaking apart.

Then you remember. The parachute has a cover and the sound you hear is the top blowing off so the parachute can be deployed.

Good, good. Now all you need to do is float down to the water—*if* you've come over the Great Lakes.

Three minutes later you feel heat. The craft is coming down. You lean forward and peer through the windshield. It is still dark. When you are about to panic, thinking that no one will see you, you see powerful searchlights crossing through the sky. They're turning back and forth, up and down—and all of a sudden, a bright light flashes in your face! Someone down there has heard the noise and is looking to see what happened.

"We're going to land!" you yell. "Save us!"

Within minutes the spacecraft splashes into dark water. It sinks, but before you have time to worry, it floats back to the surface, and you're less than fifty feet from a huge boat.

Hundreds of searchlights shine over the water. And you know someone will come get you.

The giant monkey's tail swishes back and forth. The creature's lips part, and two rows of shining teeth open and close, open and close. It is as if the animal knows you're about to be rescued . . . .

THE END

It continues walking toward you but you believe it has not realized you are nearby. It proceeds in a straight line until it is even with the first glass display— a case full of rocks that you remember the tour guide had said were from the moon's surface. The creature pauses, looks down at the display, then with one hand it lifts the whole thing from the museum floor.

You gulp. You know that the thing must weigh over 500 pounds, and this creature lifted it with one hand!

You want to creep away, and as cautiously as you can you move one foot. But the toe of your shoe catches on a broken floor tile, and you stumble.

Turn to page 55.

55

The creature whirls, still holding aloft the display case. It stares about, then looks straight down at you. Shaking all over, you stare back.

And you frown. For even in the dim light you can see through the plastic face mask, and the face within the helmet looks very familiar.

You recall all the pictures you saw during your earlier tour of the museum, and slowly one of them emerges in a special way. The guard had said very little about it, but you remember seeing something on television, a news special about one of the space lab missions. One astronaut . . .

Turn to page 70.

56

Within seconds you believe you've turned the rocket completely around. That is what you want, but the monkey seems not to like what is happening because it twists about and begins to slap at the windshield.

You don't like that! You know the windshield is strong, but if the creature keeps pounding and pounding it is liable to break. And you know what that'll mean—you'll both be sucked into space.

You wait a couple of seconds, then you hit the two retro-rocket switches. You believe that will slow down the speed of the spacecraft. You think you hear a slight explosion, and you hope that means the rockets are working.

You look at the gauges and believe the craft is slowing down. Hey, good!

But while you are congratulating yourself on selecting the proper controls, the whole spacecraft begins to rock violently back and forth. You feel yourself being thrown against the side panel, then against the monkey. And the monkey begins to scream and flick its tail back and forth.

Did you choose the wrong switches? Turn to page 65.
Did the monkey hit a different switch to cause the trouble? Turn to page 49.

You stare hard at the green light, believing that somewhere during your tour of the museum you saw something like it. You concentrate, and then you remember. The guide had told you something about using laser lights to make unusual photographs. By electronically filming an individual or an animal and exactly coordinating the pictures projected from two directions, you can obtain a three-dimensional photo. That is what this creature is. A three-dimensional . . .

Wait!

You can't be sure. For as you stare, the giant stops at the far wall, hesitates a moment, then slowly pivots. And as it does so, one of its huge arms begins to rise slowly.

In that instant you know this is more than a simple film; there's something weird and frightening about the giant's motion. You stare hard at the gloved hand at the end of the arm and realize it is holding something that looks like a special kind of gun. It is shaped like a pistol, but the barrel on the end of it has a wider than normal . . .

You swallow hard. It must be a ray gun! One that shoots a powerful beam.

If you believe it is harmless, turn to page 69.
If you think it is harmful but you can escape it, turn to page 62.

58

You know that you don't want to be in this room. The guide had pointed to this particular door and warned all visitors not to go near it, not to do so much as push at the door.

And at once you know one of the reasons why you should not be here: the odor is terrible!

You think it would be better to risk facing that weird electronic guard, and you turn back to the door. But when you feel along the surface, you find that it does not have an inside knob. And the door latched when you stepped inside. You hold your nose and wish you'd never left the motel.

But you have to get out of here!

You turn from the door and look at the far end of the room, hoping there'll be another door. There may be, but before your searching gaze can locate it, you are attracted by the workbenches along the wide aisle. This must be the design room for the mechanical and electronic experiments. On one bench, you see a mechanical device that looks like a crane arm, something that might be attached to the outside of an orbiting space station to perform lifting maneuvers. On another bench there are three coils of thin wire, designed, as well as you can tell, into a butterflylike pattern, perhaps as some kind of antenna for the spacecraft.

Turn to page 89.

You stand perfectly still, remembering that when a strange animal approaches, the safest thing is not to make a sudden move. The monkey stops beside you and stares into your face. It cocks its head and looks into your right ear. Its lips part, showing white teeth. Then suddenly it jumps straight up and lets out an ear-piercing scream. You spin about, frightened.

The monkey shakes its head, puts both its forepaws straight out, waves them slowly, then puts them on your shoulders.

And then it squeezes you!

It seems to know just where the nerve endings are, for you feel sudden, intense pain. You gradually grow numb all over, and you know that if the animal releases you, you'll fall to the floor.

It pokes its face right up to yours, its nose brushing your cheek. It snorts. Its lips open and close, open and close.

And you grow weaker!

Turn to page 96.

60

The controls are going crazy! The rocket is bouncing as if it were on a rough road, and it is about to break apart!

You scream. The monkey jerks its head about, pokes its head forward, and screams back!

But in that moment you suddenly remember something. When a spacecraft re-enters the earth's atmosphere, it is supposed to bounce about.

You try to control your hands. And as soon as you can fix your attention on the altitude dial, you watch for the needle to reach the red mark. You put your hand on the parachute switch—and the moment the needle reaches the right spot, you flick the switch.

The spacecraft suddenly trembles all over as two explosions shake everything. And you know something has gone wrong!

Is the craft breaking apart? Turn to page 52.
Is something else happening? Turn to page 11.
Or is everything going to be all right? Turn to page 67.

While you are not certain that you want to go along with the monkey, you *know* that you don't want to go back the way you came. So you follow.

The creature leads you past all the cages and turns through a narrow door. It leads you along a dim hall for several yards, then pauses, looks at you, and grins.

You stare at it, and suddenly you know this weird beast has more than an animal's mind. It is thinking! It is deliberately leading you toward something it knows about!

And you have the distinct feeling that you should not go.

Turn to page 117.

62

The guide had told you and the other visitors about all the various research projects that were an outgrowth of space and rocket activities. This, you realize, is one of them, and you are certain that if they have this kind of film showing in the museum at night, there is a good reason. This kind of guard, operated by electronics and laser beams, can do much more than a person. It can "feel" or "sense" any strangers within the museum.

And that's what you are, a stranger in the wrong place!

Before the figure can turn completely around and point you out, you decide to find an escape. Ducking low, you scamper along the wall to the first door. You grab the handle—it is long and not like all the others—and push.

And just in time. For behind you, a great flood of green light illuminates the museum. You hear two quick, sharp explosions, and the wall where you'd been hiding is no more.

But you've escaped. For now, anyway.

You let the door shut, then glance around. And you gasp. For this is the other forbidden room; this is the one with the sign over the door: AUTHORIZED PERSONNEL ONLY.

Should you go back into the passageway and hope the figure has disappeared? Turn to page 58.
Or are you curious and want to have a look around?
Turn to page 75.

But the thought is barely forming when the monkey turns its head toward you. Its mouth is open in a wide grin and it starts to chatter. And it begins to squirm about within the restraining straps. Its arms flail about, its long tail flicks right and left, and its head begins to nod back and forth.

But you don't care what it does—so long as it doesn't touch anything!

The creature's right forepaw suddenly reaches up toward a special panel of switches. It clasps one, then another of the levers beside the panel. Then all of a sudden it stops all movement.

Good, good, just stay still, you think.

But even while the idea takes shape, the monkey's right paw suddenly grabs the red lever—and jerks hard.

You feel a mild explosion beneath you. The seat is abruptly ripped from its anchor bolts. The hatch opens, and you are blown out of the spacecraft!

And your last thought is that now two humans are floating in space—the Russian cosmonaut and you . . . .

THE END

64

You wildly slap at the hatch. It does not yield. You stumble back and bump into a full-scale model of the instrument panel. You begin hitting all the buttons and jerking the levers in a desperate move.

Nothing—nothing—nothing.

Then something!

When you hit the lever with the bright orange handle, the whole lander begins to vibrate. Right below you, a rocket roars to life. Three sharp explosions follow like bolts being blown apart. The lander instantly blasts from its stand, hurling you toward the museum wall.

You yell. You grab for the hatch lock handle. You fall against the small window. But you cannot stop the wild flight.

The lander crashes against the museum wall, blasts its way through, and then abruptly stops.

The sudden halt sends you hurtling forward, and you shoot through the device's narrow roof, which opened on impact. You fall and land in the thick shrubbery that surrounds the museum.

You stay there for a moment, gulping in air. Dazed, you look about, and then you know! You've escaped from the creatures and out of the museum in that wild, crazy ride!

You do not intend to go back inside!

THE END

You don't know if you flicked the wrong switches, but you do know what is going to happen! You're going to rock back and forth, the whole rocket is going out of control, and within seconds it will plunge toward earth and burn up!

No! You don't want to burn up in space!

You reach for the rocket switches again and flick them in the opposite direction. For a moment the spacecraft continues to move violently. Then slowly it resumes its original pattern. You swallow hard and frown as you stare at the controls. You move them once again—except this time more slowly.

The spacecraft changes its position, but you feel sure it is slowing down. You study the dials, and one of them tells you that you're losing altitude. You see a red line on that dial and for a moment believe it suggests danger.

Danger? What kind of danger?

You look at the numbers, and then it dawns on you. When the needle reaches that line, you're supposed to hit the switch that opens the parachute.

But while you're studying the instrument, the monkey is again pawing the switches to its right. That is all you need—for the creature to hit the wrong one and cause the spacecraft to—

Before you can finish the thought, you feel bumpiness. You are thrown against the side of the spacecraft and realize your head is about to be banged against the hard metal.

Turn to page 60.

66

Beyond, however, there is no light, but total darkness. You hesitate, wondering what is ahead.

Then the monkey's manner changes. It stops clinging to you. It takes a quick step back. It grunts, and the sound has an angry tone. You catch your breath, wondering just what the creature intends to do.

You don't have long to wait.

With a sudden lunge, it bangs hard against you. You trip, fall forward, and before you can catch yourself the door has slammed shut behind you.

You commence to slide down a slippery passage that seems to be curved on both sides, like a huge, hollow tube. You grab wildly about, trying to catch something, anything. But your hands slide away from the wall almost as if its surface is too highly polished to catch.

Turn to page 78.

Suddenly, though, you feel a tremendous upward jerk. You think you'll fall right through the bottom of the spacecraft, but even as you feel the jolt, you smile to yourself. You know what that is. The parachute has opened and you are simply slowing your rate of descent.

You know, too, that within minutes you will land somewhere. And it had better be water.

You lean forward and stare through the windshield. You see lighted buildings, although they are a lot smaller than you thought they might be. You see lights moving about on the streets and avenues of a city.

A city? You don't want to land over a city; you want the spacecraft to come down over water. But you cannot control its path. You can do nothing but ride it down.

As it gets nearer, you begin to recognize some of the big structures from pictures you've seen. You see the— wait, now you see the tallest building in the world— the Sears Tower in Chicago.

And the spacecraft is heading for it.

There is a tall flagpole at the top.

You swallow hard. You know what is about to happen. The spacecraft is coming down right on that flagpole. You and the giant rhesus monkey will crash on top of the building . . . .

THE END

68

Not wanting to be burned alive by the robot creature, you swallow hard, yell something, and take off for the exit. You're not sure what it is, but you aren't going to hang around to find out. You stumble over a large waste container, bump against the handrail along the passageway, and dash headlong toward the door. You'll just have to wait till tomorrow and ask your father to delay the departure until you can reclaim your camera.

You get to the door and shove hard, but it does not open. You remember that when you let it shut before, you heard a click. Now you know that click meant the lock had fallen into place.

You frantically spin about. The thing—the robot in the space suit—is still stalking you.

If you believe there is another way out, turn to page 33.

If you believe that running from the robot is safest, turn to page 30.

69

You know a bit about the military weapons that designers are making, yet you don't know anything about the weapon the giant is holding. But, you tell yourself, this isn't real. What you're looking at is simply a picture—

No!

The arm continues to rise slowly until the weapon is pointed directly at the wall where you're hiding. You take a deep breath, and suddenly realize that, picture or not, there is something very sinister about the giant's posture. You cannot believe it, but it seems like he means to shoot you.

You take a step to the left. The arm moves slightly. You duck and step quickly to the right. Again the arm moves. You scream at it to stop, but the giant deliberately points the gun in your direction.

Turn to page 85.

70

But it cannot be.

The news report said that during the mission one of the astronauts went outside the vehicle to repair the experiment bay door, which had been opened and would not close properly. While he was out working with the electrical devices, one of them got tangled in his life-support cord and sent radio waves into his pulse- and brain-monitoring systems. For a short while it was feared that he was dead.

Another astronaut pulled him back inside the laboratory and used first-aid equipment inside the craft. But the astronaut lost consciousness for more than five hours, and when he was finally revived he had lost all sense of purpose or place. He went berserk, and his companion had to use strong sedation on him.

By the time he was finally brought back to earth, he had suffered irreparable damage. Genetic changes occurred, and he had become a monster.

But you thought the report said he was being kept in a special hospital in Houston, Texas.

He isn't in Houston, he is right here. You are looking at him!

Does he pose a threat? Turn to page 90.

71

The monkey leads you to the door of its cage and for a moment you think it wants you to enter. But it seems to gesture for you to stay where you are, then it leaps within. Seconds later, it returns with a half-eaten banana. It pretends to offer you a bite, jerks the food back, then eats the remainder. After the monkey swallows the food, it once more catches your hand and continues in the same direction.

You begin to understand. There is another way out of the room and that suits you fine. If you can stay away from that stalking robot astronaut, maybe you can get out safely.

The big monkey leads you through a narrow, poorly lit passge at the room's far end, then it makes a right turn. There before you is a large door with a tiny orange light above it. The animal puts your hand on the knob. You turn, and it opens freely.

And where are you? Turn to page 66.

72

You are held aloft by the robot as if you are nothing more than a rag doll. You scream, squirm, and kick, trying to free yourself. But the robot will not release you. Instead, it turns and crosses the museum, not stopping until it reaches a scaled-down radar screen. It places you against the screen, holds you there with one hand, and puts its other hand on a huge electrical switch box.

Oh, no! But you cannot move!

The robot laughs—you don't think you've ever heard such a hollow, frightening laugh—and then it jerks the switch handle.

For one brief second you feel electricity pass through you.

Suddenly you are no longer in the museum; you are whizzing through space at the speed of light. And you do not stop until you are caught in the winglike control panels of a satellite, a satellite orbiting the earth . . . .

THE END

The laser rocket suddenly explodes, and you believe the spider's poison has hit it. A cloud of smoke rises, and at the same time you feel your own numbness wearing off. Before the spider can turn on you, you dart across the floor and hide behind a large display that you remember from the tour—a display of gloves and boots worn by the astronauts.

The display, you recall, isn't simply pairs of gloves and boots, though. In the case are plaster casts of hands and feet, precisely shaped like those of one of the men. And while you are hiding there, you hear scraping noises coming from the case.

73

Has the spider found you? Turn to page 8.
Or have you simply disturbed the exhibits?
Turn to page 41.

74

You're trying to figure out the controls in the Gemini capsule.

You've only been in space for a few minutes. If you use those controls, perhaps you can make the craft come down somewhere in the United States—maybe over the Mississippi River or over one of the Great Lakes—but *somewhere* before you get over the Atlantic Ocean.

The giant rhesus is turning its head right and left, its lips parted, its teeth shining in the dim spacecraft lights. But it is ignoring you.

Fine!

Moving cautiously so you won't attract the monkey's attention, you reach for the switch that turns the craft around. You flip it and brace yourself. For a moment nothing happens and you are about to hit it again. Then you feel a slight rolling motion.

Turn to page 56.

In this top-secret room you see devices unlike anything else you've ever set your eyes on. On a large workbench is something that looks like a huge beach ball, except that it has four windmill-like propeller blades. And in the center of the ball section there is a tubular projection. You look at it more closely and tremble at what you see. In the center of the tube, shaped exactly like a rocket, is a weapon that you *know* has a nuclear warhead. A hundred space weapons like it could wipe out an entire country.

At the next bench you see something equally frightening. The "satellite" portion of the device is much like the first, a huge ball with four propeller blades. In the center of this one, however, is a collapsed reflector, and you know that when it is pushed forward and unfolded it will be a gigantic elliptical mirror, a device that will focus sun rays to destroy whole cities.

The space program is supposed to be totally peaceful, but you are certain these are weapons!

You glance around at the other items being assembled. One appears to be a rocket-launching tube much like the one on the Huey helicopter, except the rockets probably fire some sort of laser beam. Then you see what looks like an aluminum umbrella attached to a smaller, barrel-shaped satellite.

As you stare, you suddenly become aware of ticking. It is a steady ticking from one of the larger workbenches.

Is it another weapon? Turn to page 105.
Or do you believe it is just a clock? Turn to page 116.

76

It brings your hand toward its mouth, and for a moment you look at its teeth and think it is going to bite. Instead, it licks your palm.

You swallow hard and stare at it; the creature's face is almost even with yours. It makes a giggling, laughing sound as if it knows what mirth is, then it closes its fingers around your wrist. With its right forepaw, it gestures in the direction opposite from the door you entered. Then it begins to lead you that way.

To its cage? To somewhere else?

You want to pull away. Of course, there've been many times when you wanted to play with a monkey, but right now all you want to do is find your camera, get out of this very weird museum, and go back to the motel.

The monkey seems to have other plans.

Will it take you back to its cage? Turn to page 71.
Or out of the museum? Turn to page 61.

The device carries you all the way to the top, and you hear engine gears grinding. You know that within seconds you'll plummet straight down, and you cannot imagine what the fall will feel like.

But all of a sudden the grinding noises stop. In their place you hear a whooshing sound, as if air is being let out of a heavy tire. The sound slowly changes and you think it becomes a siren's whine.

Is it a signal?

But before you have time to think what it could be, you feel a sudden jolt. The release mechanism is activated, and you feel your heart is jumping into your throat, for you begin to fall!

Faster and faster you fall. You feel yourself rising off the chair and you wildly grab for its edge, anything to hold onto! Air whistles past your ear. The siren grows louder! And you yell at the top of your voice. You don't want to hit the bottom with such force!

Turn to page 107.

78

The incline becomes steeper, and you yell once more. But before you have time to do anything else, the skidding ends abruptly, and you fall straight down.

You scream and scream, just before you fall onto something soft and quite natural.

You lie there for a moment, stunned. You slowly feel about the ground. It takes several seconds, but you finally realize where you are.

Outside!

The monkey has pushed you through its own escape door to some sort of special playground. You look about. There is a tall fence, but nothing to keep you from climbing it. There are lights beyond and traffic sounds.

All you have to do is climb the fence and run, run, run to the motel.

You'll get the camera tomorrow!

THE END

And no sooner are you within the astrodome than the door slides closed and latches itself.

Well, if it opens from the outside, it'll also open from the inside, you think. Anyway, you're safe from the spider. In time it will go back to its cage, you can find your camera, then you can go back to the motel.

In the meantime you'll be comfortable.

Small lights, arranged to look like stars and planets, light the area enough for you to find the couch. You crawl onto it, sink into its comfort, and gaze up. The guide had been right. The couch moves slowly, the overhead screen also moves, and if you let yourself think about it, you do feel like you're in space.

You feel along the side of the couch, wondering if it also has controls. You touch three large round buttons and decide they have something to do with the screen and the seat. With your mind already on the "stars" above you, you absently touch the buttons. One seems to have letters engraved in it. You wonder why because no one could read it without being on the side.

You run your finger over the letters, trying to feel what they spell. One letter seems deeper than the others, and you carelessly dig your fingernail into it.

And you instantly wish that you hadn't!

For you put enough pressure on it to depress the whole button. The couch suddenly begins spinning—faster and faster. And the screen becomes a color-streaked blur.

Turn to page 108.

80

You and the giant rhesus at the controls are in a Gemini rocket heading for outer space. Through the hole in the museum ceiling, through the night, through the sky, you go.

And before you regain your full senses, before the stupor has fully worn off, you're in space. Your head aches, you feel dizzy, your stomach feels hollow, and you have this straining ache in your back. But there is nothing you can do. Nothing.

You hear the engines shut off, you feel a shattering vibration, and you know the rocket has fallen off.

Now you and the giant rhesus are floating freely in space. And you are terrified!

If you believe you can rescue yourself, turn to page 35.
If you think the monkey will do something unusual,
turn to page 9.

In that moment you feel very sorry for it. Here it is, a captive in this dimly lit room, surrounded by frogs and spiders and mice.

From the spider's cage, the monkey wanders slowly to where the oversized mouse is chewing a chunk of bread. The mouse looks up, its whiskers wiggling. The monkey cries, sounding much like a child, and springs back.

You feel more sorry for it than ever. They have no right to put it here with . . .

But before the thought is finished, the giant rhesus monkey turns again, and spies you. Bending over, its forearms waving and its mouth open, it lopes toward you.

Does it just want to play? Turn to page 15.
Or does it have something else in mind? Turn to page 59.

You involuntarily swipe at the tarantula and it falls away, this time landing on the monkey's shoulder. Surprised, the monkey jumps straight up, jabbering and chattering and waving its arms.

In that moment you spin about, leap over the nose cone of the space model, and dash for the ladder. You take the steps two at a time and grab the moon lander's hatch door. It opens and you fall inside. You quickly slide the bolt in place.

Away! You've gotten away from them and there is no way for them to get to you now that you've locked the hatch.

But there is something you hadn't counted on. This is a full-scale model, but it doesn't have all the necessary equipment. In particular, it doesn't have the oxygen supply that the astronauts used. And it is airtight.

There is no oxygen.

You quickly turn and stare out the small window to see what the monkey and spider are doing. But your line of vision is blocked by the display case of moon particles. You begin to gasp and realize that, no matter what the creatures are doing, you have to have air.

You turn back to the hatch lock and attempt to turn it. But it won't turn! You jerk and twist and struggle, but nothing you do frees it.

And you begin to cough.

Turn to page 64.

You scream because the grill is so hot your fingers are immediately blistered. You try to jerk free, but your fingertips are stuck. And you begin to feel a low electrical current passing through your body.

You are still stuck there when the robot joins you. For a moment it seems to stare down at you. Then it slowly bends over and reaches down.

You don't want it to touch you. You wish that it would just vanish, or just go back to where it was on display.

But the burning is so intense that you can't do anything to free yourself.

The robot makes a grunting noise—one that echoes because of its heavy helmet and visor. It stretches forth its huge left hand. Those harsh fingers touch your neck.

And the creature lets out the most spine-chilling scream you have ever heard. It totters back as the electrical current passing through your body sets it afire.

In that instant the grill ceases to hold your fingers. You whirl about, trip over the space capsule mounting, fall forward—and directly onto the burning robot!

And—you—burn—too . . . .

THE END

84

You frantically try to turn about and go back to the door. There *has* to be another way to escape from that robot soldier. But each time you try to turn, you begin to spin in the weightless environment. And you continue to swell.

You're getting to be a big balloon—a huge human balloon and it's no fun!

You cannot breathe, you cannot move the way you want to move, and as your eyelids keep swelling, you can no longer see.

And the last sound you make is a squeak, for you can no longer holler either, before you completely explode . . . .

THE END

You frantically look to the other side of the museum where the green light is, but there is no help for you from that direction. Rather, the beam glows brighter.

Once more you scream out. You drop to your knees, while your hands wildly search the floor, then you fall prone and begin to roll.

But there is no way of escaping. You see the brightness increase. You feel heat beginning to build up around you. And even as you try to roll away, the beam finds your prone body.

There is a sudden flash, as if the entire museum is aglow with a thousand spotlights. You feel one quick, terribly burning sensation. You gasp for breath. But you are already paralyzed . . . .

THE END

87

With this strange whistling noise the vibrations stop. The monkey becomes very still. A green light flicks on and off, on and off. That stops, and a red light begins to flicker.

Then you hear a hissing noise. Sparks fly from the panel, which the monkey hit moments earlier. You smell something very peculiar—it smells like burning rubber.

You look wildly about. You see nothing, but the smell gets worse. And the hissing noise turns into a gurgling, popping sound—like frying bacon.

You swallow hard because you think you know what the noise and smell mean. There is a fire behind the panel!

Terrified, you try to reach for it, but it is just beyond the tips of your fingers. You think maybe there is a fire extinguisher aboard. But where? Where?

You want to feel under the seat, but you do not have a chance.

For suddenly the sizzling sound becomes a soft roar. Flames erupt from the panel, and the whole spacecraft explodes!

You really didn't need your camera, anyway—not where you'll be for the rest of your very short life . . . .

THE END

88

The chair begins to shake violently, and you're sure you've set the elevator device in motion. But you don't want to go up to the top and take that wild plunge down at 100 mph! You don't want to do anything but stay away from that huge spider!

You grab the second control and work it back and forth. Nothing happens. You work it harder—and suddenly the chair seems to drop straight down.

The guide had said nothing about the thing going down!

But it does, and within half a second, you're at a level below the main museum floor. The small door flies open, and you fall out. You scramble to your feet, wondering where you are. At first you think you're in a simple basement and you relax. But before you have time to take a good deep breath, you hear the roar of heavy turbine engines. You're in the main power plant of the museum, and those turbines are the electrical generators.

But it is totally dark, and no one is near!

Turn to page 112.

89

As you continue to gaze around this mechanical/ electrical design room, you notice something even more interesting.

Standing off by itself, as if it had special value, is an upright box that reminds you of a telephone booth, except that it has more wires than most telephone booths usually have and you . . .

Wait, now. Hey, that's an idea. It *is* a telephone booth—a special kind that is radio-equipped. Those wires are just the radio connections.

And the thought makes you almost laugh. Maybe you cannot find a safe way out of this museum. But all you have to do is go over there, call the motel, ring your room, and tell your father to come get you. He'll probably fuss at you for slipping away, but a little fussing is a lot better than being trapped here.

You cross to it, hesitate only a moment, and pull open the narrow door.

Turn to page 110.

90

And now the monstrous astronaut is staring at you. At first there appears to be a puzzled expression on his face. Then it disappears. In its place is a look of horrifying anger. He yells! And the sound is like the roar of a rocket being ignited. The walls of the museum seem to vibrate. He raises the display case even higher, holds it aloft a moment, then he hurls it in your direction. "Lunar thing, lunar thing, lunar thing!" he screams.

You roll hard to the left, scrambling as fast as you can to dodge the huge object. But it is much larger than you are, and you cannot escape. It comes crashing down on you. And the last thing you hear is the cry of the crazed astronaut: "In space there is lunar waste!"

You don't know what that means. But you are beyond caring . . . .

THE END

Sitting in this cramped space vehicle with your arms caught is making you feel more desperate by the minute.

You feel about with your feet and find three pedal controls. You can't be sure what they're for, but since the vehicle is mounted on something other than a live rocket launcher, you think you can push one and do no damage.

You hesitate for a moment, then you hear the "robot" coming into the main area of the museum. You take a deep breath, hold it, and kick the left pedal.

It does *not* do what you'd hoped.

If you believe you've put yourself in danger, turn to page 43.
If you believe the act has saved you from harm, turn to page 25.

92

You're in the mock-up of the *Vostok* trying to calm down when . . .

Oh, no!

Just as you are about to relax, you hear heavy pounding at the small door you entered. The robot has climbed the ladder and is right outside.

You're terrified. If it can climb the ladder, it can do almost anything. You turn around, looking at the opposite side of the Russian space ship, hoping there is another way out. You see nothing except a small window. It is high off the museum floor, and you could get hurt if you jump out, but that's better than getting burned to death by those sparks from the space robot's long fingers.

Again the robot bangs on the door—and it begins to open!

Turn to page 101.

93

And you are instantly hypnotized by this vicious and grotesque spider, which has somehow been dreadfully changed during its experimental journey into space.

You are able to see. You are able to think. You know what is going on. But you can do nothing!

As if enjoying your condition, the giant rhesus begins to hop up and down. Its mouth opens and shuts, opens and shuts. It bounds toward you, jabbering as it approaches, and grabs you by the neck. It lifts you easily.

Turn to page 95.

The monstrous monkey carries you back to the room where you found it, with the sinister spider scurrying along at its side.

The monkey takes you directly to the spider's cage, turns about, and deposits you unceremoniously on the cage floor. You look wildly about, hearing little scratching noises coming from a corner of the cage. You stare toward the sound.

There, creeping toward you, are six smaller tarantulas—offspring of the huge one. And you know that you are to be their next meal . . . .

THE END

96

Your knees buckle. Your arms grow limp. You try to take a deep breath but the pain is now so intense you cannot. And within seconds you slump to the floor.

The giant rhesus squats as you fall, still clinging to your shoulders. And it does not release its hold until you are lying flat on your back. When you are almost unconscious, wondering *why* this is happening, the creature grabs you by your feet and commences to drag you down the passageway toward its large cage. It lifts you, and shoves you through its cage door. Inside, it pushes you against the corner and covers you with a horrible-smelling blanket.

You know you will choke and that the fumes from the blanket will keep you from breathing. And you know you do not have enough strength to move it away from you.

In the morning someone will come to feed the animal. He or she will discover you lying inside. But by then you will have been suffocated . . . .

THE END

Your heart begins to race and you *know* you've entered into the wrong room. You whirl about and are ready to run when you hear a sharp, crackling noise.

You spin. The mad scientist, and there is no other word for him, is holding something that looks like a long flashlight with an oversized reflector. It is glowing red, and you stare into it.

The crackling noise comes once more. The head of the flashlight glows even redder, and you feel a stinging sensation pass through your body.

You tremble all over. Whoever or whatever he is, he is aiming that thing straight at you. You know, you just know, it produces high-voltage electricity. That is causing the stinging—an electrical shock!

Turn to page 109.

98

You are thinking about what the guide had said, staring at the door, when you hear a whispery, scraping noise—as if something is being brushed over the floor.

The spider! It has discovered where you are and is crawling toward you! Without hesitating, you grab the column's door handle and jerk it open. You scamper inside, shut the door, and breathe a sigh of relief because you know the spider cannot get inside.

You realize, though, that except for one tiny light all the way at the top of the column, you're in darkness. You ease into the reclining chair, lean back, and decide that you'll just wait there for a while. Sooner or later the spider will give up.

You let your eyes grow accustomed to the almost total darkness, then you glance about. To the left you see two heavy, coiled springs, which are probably used to reduce the sudden shock when the astronaut comes down. To the right you see two switches. They're small and oddly shaped, and you let your hand feel their surfaces.

Just at that moment you hear a scraping noise against the door, and the shock of the noise makes you shiver all over.

Your right hand jerks—and you pull one of the levers!

If you think the door pops open, turn to page 88.
If you believe something else will happen, turn to page 106.

Before the stranger can spot you, you dart around the first display case you come to and squat down. From your hidden spot you peer out.

The figure is dressed in a uniform, all right, but it does not look like that of a guard. Instead, you remember the display of rocket soldiers at the far side of the museum. Dressed in combat gear, the figures were holding small rocket launchers. And that is just what this one coming your way has in his hand: a heat-seeking rocket he can easily fire from the shouldered combat launcher.

Are you about to become a combat target? Turn to page 47.
If you believe you can avoid being seen, turn to page 26.

100

And the bees must have changed, too!

The sign says DANGER!

But before you have time to do more than turn half about, the giant rhesus monkey laughs, then it opens the cage door.

The buzzing becomes ferociously loud. You want to spin around and run!

But before you can do so, the monkey pushes you into the cage and slams the opening shut!

You fall inside, and the dangerous bees at once swarm all over you. You scream and scream as they begin to sting. But within seconds your screaming stops. And you feel nothing . . . .

THE END

The robot bangs even harder on the door of the *Vostok* and now it is almost half open.

Trembling all over, you start toward the window, but you don't look where you're going. Your foot bumps against something on the side of the mockup—and all of a sudden the spacecraft begins to vibrate. Slowly it tilts upward. You fall back against the door where the robot is. The door pops the rest of the way open—and you fall against the creature!

It grabs you but the ladder falls. You and the robot tumble to the museum floor. You are all right, but the robot is smashed to pieces. And yet it screams! The sound is deafening.

But the robot can no longer stalk you. As its helmeted head rolls away, you spin around, kick it, and run toward the theater. Dashing to the right seat, you grab your camera and scurry back to the main door. This time, instead of trying the handle, you bang your shoulder against it—and it crashes open.

And you're out of that terrifying museum . . . .

THE END

102

Your head is hurting, you can't stop screaming, and you're desperately trying to free your arms.

Finally you release the lever, you take your thumb off the button, and you grip the armrests with both hands. The capsule slowly stops bouncing. Soon, you think it will be still again—and then you can try something else to free your arms.

But just as the capsule stops all movement, you sense something close to you. You turn. You stare through the windshield opening and look directly into the robot's eyes, which are made larger by the thick green visor! It reaches both hands inside and grips its coarse, gloved fingers on your shoulders. It lifts you up so hard that the metal straps binding your arms snap.

Turn to page 72.

103

And the concrete disintegrates, crumbling to the museum floor as nothing more than bits of gravel and grains of sand!

You don't believe anything can do that, but it just did!

Screaming, "Don't shoot again!" you stand and raise your arms. Your knees are shaking, your throat is dry, and you are trembling all over.

But the robot soldier cannot hear. It can only fire its heat-seeking rocket.

You see its finger close on the trigger. You see the quick burst of fire from the launcher tube. And as the rocket zooms toward you, you know that is the very last thing you'll ever see . . . .

THE END

104

Seconds after the soldier dummy evaporates, the spider returns, grasps the monkey's paw once more, and the three of you continue across the museum floor.

Those two lead you down a narrow walkway and stop beside what the guide had told you was a small-scale version of one of the Gemini rockets, complete with its two-man capsule. Although it is not as large as the real one, it is still more than twenty feet long. And although it is lying horizontally, it is supported by the same kind of machinery that supported the real launch rocket and space vehicle during one of the missions, gantry and all.

You gulp as you stare at the device, because you believe the monkey and spider have brought you here for a purpose.

If you believe they have a definite plan, turn to page 48.

If you think now is the time to attempt an escape, turn to page 22.

105

You spin about and stare in the direction of the sound, discovering to your horror that you are not alone. The sound comes from a digital measuring device. And using it as he sits behind one of the larger workbenches is a very old midget-sized man with stringy gray hair, a sparse beard, and thick glasses. He peers at you, and you realize he has been watching you all the time you've been in the room. Only when you stare at him does he speak. "NO ONE EVER ENTERS THIS ROOM!" The voice is high-pitched and quivery, but very fierce and very frightening.

Turn to page 118.

The seat begins to vibrate. And before you can stop it, the thing begins to rise slowly.

You jerk your hand away from the levers, thinking that if you don't touch it again it will stop. But the chair keeps moving up.

You've set it in motion, but you don't remember what the guide had said about stopping it. You don't think he even had mentioned anything about it!

You rise and rise—and within moments you know you'll be at the top. You are afraid that once it gets there, the release mechanism will work and you'll fall straight down at a speed of 100 mph!

You scream! You twist right and left. But you don't want to twist too much because if you slip out of the chair you'll fall without any cushioning—and you don't know what lies beneath the chair rest.

Turn to page 77.

But nothing stops you. Nothing even slows you as you plunge down and down . . . .

Toward what?

10

The guide had said something about the machine stopping abruptly as it reached bottom. But you sense that something isn't working as it should. Perhaps it is because the museum's power equipment is not completely functioning. After all, it is nearly midnight. Or perhaps there is another control you should use, but you don't know which one.

The speed takes your breath away as you barely stay on the chair. It seems to be falling faster than you are. If . . .

Suddenly, though, you slam hard against the bottom. You think you're being mashed flat. You are about to relax when suddenly the chair begins to vibrate all over. You try to roll out of it but you cannot. The siren starts again, and then something blows up! The chair begins to spin violently. You are thrown against the door. It crashes open.

And there, waiting for you, is the gigantic tarantula. As you sprawl across the floor, the creature springs at you.

And it knows exactly where and how to bite . . . .

THE END

08

You wildly press the other two buttons. One causes brilliant lights to flash on and off, on and off. The other raises the couch. You yell and cry out, but the guide had said this astrodome is soundproof. No one could hear you even if they were right outside the exhibit.

The couch begins to whirl. The overhead screen spins faster, and as you try to make the machines stop, you find yourself getting dizzier and dizzier. You grab the couch's sides, but its cover is a slick vinyl and you can't get a good grip. You attempt to turn over but you cannot. Finally, you draw yourself up into a ball, take a deep breath, and roll as hard to the left as you can.

You fall off the couch and drop into some electrical wires. Sparks fly, and even as you wish you'd stayed at the motel, you're zapped upward. Toward the revolving screen. Toward the largest star. Toward space. And as the electrical current sizzles through your body, you think you'll be on that star-swept screen forever . . . .

THE END

So that is what they're doing with these animals. They're testing them with various kinds of electrical devices to see what they can stand before they use the same devices on the astronauts.

Or are these things fantastic new weapons?
You don't know! You don't want to know! All you want to do is run away . . .

But before you can even finish the thought, the scientist holds the flashlight weapon out, grins a crazy grin, and fires the device once more.

The sting becomes a violent burn, and your body seems on fire. As you slump to the floor—you know—it is—some kind—of ve-ry—new—weapon. And you—know—you won't—ever escape . . . .

THE END

10

You step through the little opening and let the door swing shut. It closes with three quick clicks, and you spin about to stare at it. No telephone booth has three locks. But you shrug your shoulders and think this is something very new. Maybe the engineers just like three locks.

You look about for the telephone, but instead of an instrument, you see a switch panel. You stare at it for a moment, then turn all the way around. There, opposite the switch panel, are four narrow strips of metal that reach from top to bottom. And they are gleaming.

It must be a totally new kind of telephone. You press the numbers on the panel, the mechanism rings, and those metal strips let you talk and hear without holding an instrument.

You smile as you press the main button on the panel. At once you hear a hum, and suddenly you have a frightening thought. This is not a telephone. It is one of those future-transport devices, a way of making people travel great distances by changing them into electronic waves!

The hum gets louder. You feel heat from those narrow strips of metal. You also feel yourself shrinking. You get shorter and smaller. And just as you realize what is happening, you completely disappear from the booth. You're an electronic wave being transmitted. But there is no receiving device because the engineers have provided only the sender . . . .

THE END

While in motion you try taking a step, and you manage to move halfway across the room. Actually you are floating! You take another step, and you float all the way to the far wall. This is an anti-gravity device with very low gravity so the astronauts who went to the moon could know what to expect on its surface.

For a moment you are relieved to be away from that robot soldier. And for that same moment the idea of being weightless appeals to you. But before you have time to enjoy the feeling, you think you are beginning to swell. Your stomach seems to be getting much bigger, and you feel your skin stretching. And all at once you know why.

You're in a near vacuum. To create this device, the engineers have taken all the air out of it. And the pressure within your body makes you swell up. *You don't like it!*

Turn to page 84.

112

In the darkness you stagger to your feet and slowly feel about. You touch a huge drum-shaped machine, and jerk your hand away. It is too hot to touch. You step to the left, feel about, and find what you think is the rail along stairs. Good. You'll just climb them, find the door, and . . .

But the rail runs along something else, something quite different. It is a conveyor belt going up. You bend close, trying to decide whether to get on it or not. But before you can decide, an overhead boom decides for you! It knocks you forward and you sprawl onto the belt.

You don't want to ride! You don't want to go back up into the museum. All you want to do is get away . . . .

But you cling to the belt to keep from falling onto the hot machinery. The rollers hum, the belt speeds, and all of a sudden you're sent crashing through double swinging doors and the belt flings you up and out.

You fall onto soft, grassy earth, and then you understand. The conveyor belt carries garbage outside. You get up and start running. You crash into garbage cans but you don't care. You're out, really out . . . .

THE END

113

The helicopter will strike the ceiling!

Within seconds it does just that. It crashes hard, and all at once fire begins to spurt from the engine. The craft totters right and left, then plunges toward the museum floor. You yell—you scream—and grab for something in an effort to climb out before it crashes.

You catch a large lever and jerk it, and suddenly the rockets begin to go off. They strike the Apollo spacecraft—the very one in which three astronauts rode to the moon. One strikes the huge telescope mock-up and synthetic stars flash all about. Another rocket strikes the replica of the Russian *Vostok,* knocking it down. And another hits the cage where the small rhesus monkey is.

Turn to page 115.

One of the rockets also strikes the far wall of the museum. It bursts into flame, and as it burns you are certain that you will never be able to escape—because you're now pinned inside the cabin of the flaming gunship . . . .

THE END

Trembling all over, you whirl about and stare in the direction of the sound. You see a large red device that looks like a television screen. Small numbers flash on it in rapid sequence. The thing ticks at even intervals. You watch a moment, and all of a sudden the numbers disappear. In their place appears the helmeted head of an astronaut. Except that visible through the visor is a face that looks like a purple-eyed monster. And as you stare, the head slowly comes out of the screen and takes full shape. You know you are looking at something that must have been brought back from outer space.

Suddenly, you hear a laugh, but it comes from a speaker overhead. You glance in that direction, and a very clear voice says, "Go to the rear! There's another door! But don't ever come here again!"

The voice dies away. And when you look back at the figure, it has receded into the television screen. It fades, and the numbers return.

You don't wait for a second invitation! Never mind the camera, you'll get it tomorrow! Ignoring the work benches, you dash toward the rear. Sure enough, there is a regular door. You push the handle, scurry through, and you're outside the museum! And you see that you are not far from the motel . . . .

THE END

As if sensing your uncertainty, the creature gives your hand a harsh squeeze, then jerks you about. It forces you to turn the corner and follow down an even narrower hall. And as you move along it, you begin to hear buzzing noises. With each step you take, the noises get louder.

You come to another sharp turn in the hall, and the monkey leads you to a narrow, heavily screened cage opening. It steps to the side and you glance at the large placard attached to the cage: SPACE BEES—DANGER—PROTECTIVE CLOTHING ESSENTIAL!

Space bees! You don't know about space bees, but you quickly guess that they've also been taken on one of the space laboratory missions . . . .

Turn to page 100.

118

You start to explain why you've entered, but the old man violently jerks up one of the tools before him. It looks like a small bicycle-tire pump, but you know it cannot be that. It must be some kind of weapon. You yell at him not to use it, but he ignores you. He points it at you and pulls back the plunger.

You scream again!

He laughs a chattery, coughing laugh. But there is no mirth in the sound. He points, he aims, and with a sudden motion he rams the plunger into the device.

Sparks fly from the end of the device's barrel. A force strikes you violently in the middle of the forehead. You attempt to put your hand to the spot, but suddenly you are paralyzed.

"NO ONE EVER ENTERS THIS ROOM!" the old man screams again.

As you slump to the floor, you know those are the last words you'll ever hear . . . .

THE END